Disney Peter Pan

The Lost Bear

Never Land is a place full of magic and mischief, especially when a certain little pixie is around! Read along as Tinker Bell and Peter Pan go on a journey to help a friend. You'll know it's time to turn the page when you hear this sound....Are you ready? Here we go!

publications international, ltd.

Stars are still twinkling in the sky as Tinker Bell and Peter Pan leave Never Land to fly the Darlings back home.

"Thank you for a wonderful adventure," says Wendy Darling to her magical friends. Along with her brothers John and Michael, Wendy has braved a slingshot attack, fought off pirates, and rescued the daughter of an Indian chief — all before bedtime.

As she flies through the window of the nursery, Wendy looks forward to a peaceful night's sleep.

"Time for bed!" Wendy says to her younger brothers. "I'll tell you a story."

Peter Pan would like to hear one of Wendy's stories, because they are always about him. But Michael and John are too excited from their adventure to settle down just yet.

"Let's play pirates!" says John. "I'll be Captain Hook." Michael eagerly hops up onto a dresser and draws his toy sword.

At last, Wendy manages to tuck Michael into bed. But when he looks for his teddy bear... it's nowhere to be found!

Wendy searches every nook in the nursery. There is no sign of Bear. Sadly Michael shuts his eyes. It will be hard for him to fall asleep without his beloved bear by his side.

Tinker Bell wonders if Michael left his teddy bear in Never Land. Peter Pan thinks he probably did. So with a sprinkling of pixie dust, Tink and Peter magically fly back to Never Land to look for Bear.

"Where should we start, Tink?" Peter Pan asks. "Pirate's Cove? Mermaid Lagoon? Skull Rock? The Indian Camp?"

Tinker Bell has an idea. Six of them, in fact. She flies straight towards Peter Pan's hideout in Hangman's Tree. The six Lost Boys are there, and she wonders if any of them have, by chance, seen Michael's bear.

"Hmmm," says one of the Lost Boys. "Come to think of it, I have seen a bear. One of the pirates grabbed it when they captured us!"

"I've seen a bear too!" says another Lost Boy. "One of the Indians grabbed it when *they* captured us!"

Suddenly, clear as a bell, Tink remembers the last time *she* saw the bear. Michael was clutching it on the way back home. And she's quite sure of it, because he was clutching her as well!

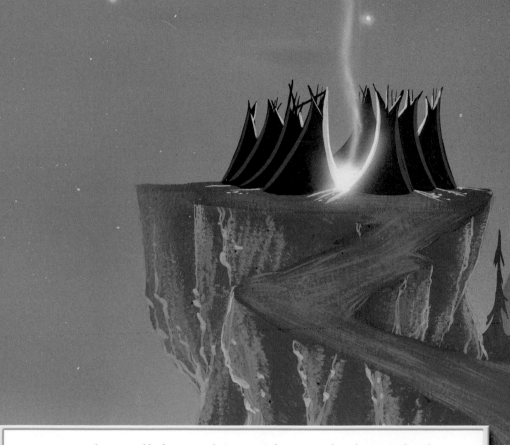

Now Tinker Bell doesn't know where to look. Perched thoughtfully on a leaf, she turns over possibilities in her mind. The lost bear has got to be somewhere. But if it's not in Never Land, and it's nowhere to be seen in the nursery, then where?

It's a mystery, all right. If only she had the key...

But that's it! Quick as a wink, Tink flies off to find Peter Pan.

Peter Pan has been busy coming up with his own solution to the lost bear problem.

"Look, Tink!" he says, as the little pixie zooms into Peter's hideout. "If we can't find Michael's bear — and it doesn't seem we can — then we can bring him a brand-new bear. Do you think he'll like it?"

But Tinker Bell just tugs the box's fancy bow and urges Peter to come along with her.

"Where are we going?" Peter Pan asks, bewildered. But before he can find out, Tinker Bell is off in a flash of pixie dust. Peter has to fly doubly fast to keep up. Soon Never Land is just a speck in the distance, and Tink and Peter have reached the rooftop of the Darlings' house.

Quietly, Peter Pan follows Tinker Bell in through the nursery window.

"Tink, I don't understand," says Peter Pan. "Wendy already searched everywhere in the nursery."

Tinker Bell shakes her head and flies to the dresser drawer. Then she squeezes herself through the tiny key hole. Peter hears her fiddling with the lock. Suddenly the drawer pops open, and there is Tink — with Michael's treasured teddy bear!

"He must have dropped it in there when he was playing pirates with John!" Peter exclaims.

"Well done, Tink!" says Peter Pan. "Let's tell everyone the good news!"

Tinker Bell sprinkles some pixie dust on the Darlings. Wendy and John hop right out of bed. Michael stands up slowly and rubs his sleepy little head.

"Tink found Michael's bear right there in the drawer!"
Peter blurts out. "We woke you all up to tell you, so you
could get some sleep!"

Moments later, the door to the nursery opens ever so slightly. Mrs. Darling peeks in to see what all the commotion is. But all she sees are Wendy, John, and Michael in their beds, fast asleep. She smooths out Wendy's blanket, gives John a little kiss, and tucks Michael and his teddy bear in, extra tight.

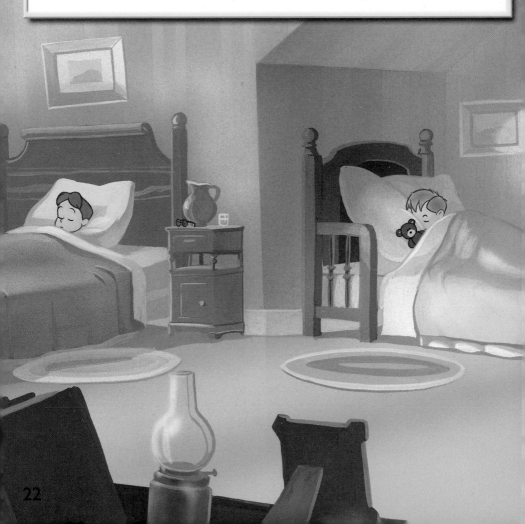

Then she shuts the window to keep out the draft, or anything else that might fly in through a window at night.

High above the house, the stars are just about ready to stop twinkling and let the morning sun take its place in the sky.

Tinker Bell and Peter Pan are well on their way back to Never Land.